MW00884178

This book belongs to

_____

Hallie & Grace

in the beginning, God...

jan johnson

In the beginning, God...

Dear Parents,

We are truly excited to share with you and your child, *Hallie and Grace—In the beginning, God . . .* It is our hope that this book will play a part in the building of your child's confidence and sense of worth by pointing them to the One who created and loves them—our Lord and Savior, Jesus Christ. All children are a gift from God and a precious responsibility, and we believe, as parents, we are accountable to God for the way we choose to bring them up. We are responsible to bring them up in truth and love and pray that they will have hearts that seek after God.

In a world that tells your little ones that their value is external, the characters of Hallie and Grace show them through the Word of God that it is through the eyes of God that we can see our true worth. We pray that you will not only grow closer to your children as you share this story, but most importantly, we pray that you and your child will grow closer to your Heavenly Father. When you draw your strength and confidence as a parent from Jesus Christ, then your children can learn to do the same.

May God bless you and your family.

Love in Christ,
Jan & Pat

Dedication

Pat Weaver—Living proof that God still moves mountains.

Madison and Makenzie—God's divine designs and my inspiration.

Herb—Still in love with you after all these years.

"You made my whole being. You formed me in my mother's body. I praise you because you made me in an amazing and wonderful way. What you have done is wonderful. I know this very well. You saw my bones being formed as I took shape in my mother's body. When I was put together there, you saw my body as if it was formed. All the days planned for me were written in your book before I was one day old" (Psalm 139:13–16).

Wow, that was a pretty good way to start my life. I guess I must be somebody important for God, Himself, to make me

and then call it wonderful before I was ever even born.

God had a really big surprise for my mom and dad when He made me, because He made my sister, Grace, at the same time.

You see, Grace and I are twins.

I'm Hallie

My grandma remembers the day she went to the doctor with my mom before we were born. They saw a picture of Grace and me with a machine they call an ultrasound. It can take a picture right through your tummy. I don't think it hurt.

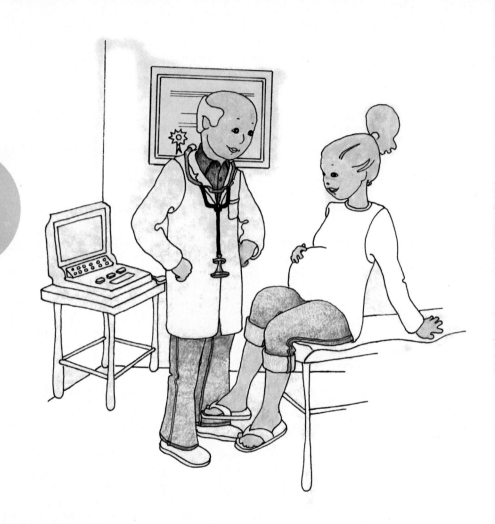

They could see our fingers and toes and eyes and nose, and we moved around a lot. Grandma says we still look just like our ultrasound pictures.

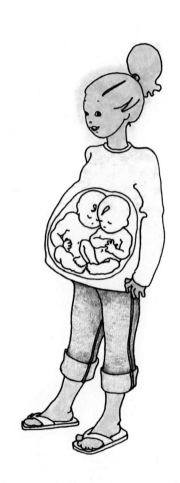

God says He could see us, too, but He did not need a machine. He can see right through your tummy too.

I think He recognized Grace and me right away.

It makes me feel very happy that God knows so much about Grace and me.

I guess it makes us each someone very special.

Did you know that God made you too?

e|LIVE

listen|imagine|view|experience

AUDIO BOOK DOWNLOAD INCLUDED WITH THIS BOOK!

In your hands you hold a complete digital entertainment package. Besides purchasing the paper version of this book, this book includes a free download of the audio version of this book. Simply use the code listed below when visiting our website. Once downloaded to your computer, you can listen to the book through your computer's speakers, burn it to an audio CD or save the file to your portable music device (such as Apple's popular iPod) and listen on the go!

How to get your free audio book digital download:

1. Visit www.tatepublishing.com and click on the e|LIVE logo on the home page.
2. Enter the following coupon code:
   e1ad-9ef5-dfae-fa81-04c9-ed71-2cc0-32fc
3. Download the audio book from your e|LIVE digital locker and begin enjoying your new digital entertainment package today!